Hattie B
Magical Vet

The Fairy's Wing

CLAIRE TAYLOR-SMITH

Illustrated by Lorena Alvarez

PUFFIN

PUFFIN BOOKS

Published by the Penguin Group
Penguin Books Ltd, 80 Strand, London WC2R ORL, England
Penguin Group (USA) Inc., 375 Hudson Street, New York, New York 10014, USA
Penguin Group (Canada), 90 Eglinton Avenue East, Suite 700, Toronto, Ontario, Canada M4P 2Y3
(a division of Pearson Penguin Canada Inc.)
Penguin Ireland, 25 St Stephen's Green, Dublin 2, Ireland (a division of Penguin Books Ltd)
Penguin Group (Australia), 707 Collins Street, Melbourne, Victoria 3008, Australia
(a division of Pearson Australia Group Pty Ltd)
Penguin Books India Pvt Ltd, 11 Community Centre, Panchsheel Park, New Delhi – 110 017, India
Penguin Group (NZ), 67 Apollo Drive, Rosedale, Auckland 0632, New Zealand
(a division of Pearson New Zealand Ltd)
Penguin Books (South Africa) (Pty) Ltd, Block D, Rosebank Office Park,
181 Jan Smuts Avenue, Parktown North, Gauteng 2193, South Africa

Penguin Books Ltd, Registered Offices: 80 Strand, London WC2R ORL, England

puffinbooks.com

First published 2014
001

Text and illustrations copyright © Penguin Books Ltd, 2014
Story concept originated by Mums Creative Content Ltd
Illustrations by Lorena Alvarez
With thanks to Claire Baker
All rights reserved

The moral right of the copyright holders and illustrator has been asserted

Set in 14.5/24 pt Bembo Book MT Std
Typeset by Jouve (UK), Milton Keynes
Printed in Great Britain by Clays Ltd, St Ives plc

British Library Cataloguing in Publication Data
A CIP catalogue record for this book is available from the British Library

ISBN: 978-0-141-34468-3

www.greenpenguin.co.uk

Love forever to Nana Jenny,

our brightest Star in the Sky

xxx

Love always to Grandma Peggy,

for her constant encouragement,

excitement and love

xxx

Winter
Mountains

Cave

Valley
of the
Guardians

Pixie
Park

Elf
Avenue

Dragon's
Valley

Silvery Stream

Unicorn
Meadows

Enchanted
Orchard

Rumbling
Volcano

Troll
Bridge

Fairy Forest

Rainbow
Waterfall

Ancient
Desert

Hidden
Lake

Frozen
Merlakes

Contents

A Touch of Trouble

The bell that signalled the start of another week of school had just rung and Hattie Bright joined the queue of pupils filing into the classroom. She was clutching a small box, which was taped down on all four sides.

Hattie's best friend, Chloe, joined her in the line. 'What did you bring in for the history

project then?' she asked, looking at the box
curiously.

'A little china pot that my mum has on her
dressing table,' replied Hattie. 'It's got two
handles and pretty blue flowers all over it. She

keeps bracelets and things in it. It used to belong to my grandma, but Mum said I could bring it in as long as I'm *really* careful.'

'You're lucky your mum let you bring it at all,' said Chloe. 'I don't think my parents would trust me with something that delicate – I'm so clumsy! When I told my dad I had to bring something in that had been passed down from an older generation, all he would dig out was this old atlas. I think it was my grandpa's. It's so dusty!'

Hattie peered at the old book poking out from under Chloe's arm and laughed in agreement.

'Oh well,' said Chloe as the two girls headed through the door, 'at least we've both brought something in.'

In the classroom, the display was already taking shape. Mr Neal had covered a long table with an old lace tablecloth and Hattie's classmates were placing a variety of items on it. There were toys, photographs, a shiny metal whistle and even tickets to a football match held in the 1960s!

While Chloe went off to clean her atlas, Hattie carefully removed the pot from the box. She'd just taken it out of the tissue paper it had been wrapped in for protection when she heard the swish of fabric behind her, quickly followed by the sickly sweet voice of her mean classmate Victoria Frost as she spoke to her two sidekicks.

'Where shall I put this then? I don't think it'll fit on that little table, do you, Jodie? Louisa, can you see anywhere I can hang it up?'

Hattie turned to see Victoria holding up a spectacular wedding dress. She couldn't help but have a long look at it, taking in the thick creamy satin fabric, the pretty crystal beads sewn round the neckline and the panels of lace leading from the fitted top to the flowing skirt.

'It's beautiful, isn't it?' said Victoria, noticing Hattie's admiring gaze. 'It belonged to my grandmother. She wore it for her wedding, then she passed it on to my mum so she could

wear it when she married my dad. I expect I'll get to wear it too one day,' she added, holding it against her.

'Oh, you'll *definitely* get married. Who wouldn't want to marry you?' said Jodie, and Louisa nodded her head in agreement.

Victoria beamed at her simpering sidekicks. 'Ask Mr Neal where I can hang it, will you?' She barked her order at Jodie, who scurried off with Louisa. Victoria then turned her attention back to Hattie, who was placing her mum's pot on the table, next to a purple bead necklace. 'What did you bring in, Hattie – that funny little thing? Why on earth would anyone pass *that* on? I mean, it can't exactly be worth much.

This dress is an antique. It must be worth thousands of pounds now!'

Hattie felt her blood begin to rise. Why did Victoria have to be so nasty about *everything*? And why did she always have to be better than everyone else? Hattie clenched her teeth, before remembering that Victoria wasn't *always* the best at everything. Hadn't Hattie beaten her in that swimming race not so long ago? The one where everyone had cheered her to victory while Victoria had been left shaking with fury?

The memory made Hattie feel braver. She swung away from the display table to face Victoria and tell her exactly what she thought of her stupid wedding dress. But, as she did so, her elbow caught the little china pot. It all happened so fast, yet to Hattie it felt as if she was watching in slow motion: first the pot tipped to one side, then the other, and then it wobbled more, before finally falling over and landing on its side with a *clink*. Victoria let out a spiteful snort and Hattie reached for it with a feeling of dread.

As soon as she picked it up, Hattie knew she was in big trouble. Horrified, she saw that one of its delicate handles had broken off.

'Oops!' said Victoria with a sneer. She walked away, leaving Hattie to scoop up the handle.

Chloe came back over. 'What's happened?'

she asked, looking at Hattie with concern. Spotting a smirking Victoria nearby, she added, 'It wasn't vile Victoria being mean again, was it?'

Hattie didn't answer. Instead, she held out the handle on her palm.

'Did Victoria –'

Hattie didn't give Chloe a chance to finish her question. 'Victoria's mean but *she* didn't break it – *I* did!' said Hattie. 'I knocked it over and now it's broken. My mum's going to go absolutely crazy!'

Chloe put a friendly arm round Hattie's shoulders. 'I'm sure she'll understand,' she said, leaning in to peer more closely at the piece of china. 'It looks like a clean break. I don't think it'll be too hard to fix with some glue.'

Hattie wished she shared Chloe's confidence, but Mum had trusted her to look after the pot and, with the school day barely even started, she'd already broken it! She sighed. 'I'm going to be in so much trouble!'

At the end of the day Hattie was anxious to get home as quickly as possible. She was hurrying past the village Post Office when she heard someone call her name.

'Hattie! Hello!'

Hattie recognized the voice immediately. 'Uncle B!' she cried, delighted and surprised to see him again. 'What are you doing here?'

'Well, um, posting a letter of course,' he replied, indicating the Post Office behind him.

Hattie loved bumping into Uncle B. He was the only one that knew her secret – that she was the Guardian of the magical Kingdom of Bellua and all its creatures. And he was the only one that could understand her adventures as he'd been the Guardian before her.

'And what might my favourite niece have in that precious-looking box?' asked Uncle B, pointing at the parcel that Hattie was clutching tightly.

Hattie's heart sank. Should she tell him about the broken pot? One look at her uncle's friendly face made up her mind. 'Oh, Uncle B, I've had a disaster!' she said.

'Tell me what happened,' said Uncle B kindly.

Hattie's words tumbled out in a great rush. 'Well, Mum let me take her antique pot to school for our history project, but when I put it on the display table in our classroom I sort of knocked into it and . . . and . . . it fell over and one of the handles came off. I feel terrible and I don't know how I'm going to tell Mum!'

To her surprise, Uncle B was smiling as she finished her story. 'Don't worry, Hattie,' he said. 'I'm sure it will be OK. Problems like this tend to fix themselves, you know. Very often help comes from the most unexpected of places. Good luck!' And, with that, he patted

Hattie lightly on the arm, called a bright 'Cheerio!' and headed off towards the village green, chuckling to himself.

What a strange thing to say, thought Hattie as she set off in the opposite direction. Although she had no idea where this unexpected help might come from, she really hoped Uncle B was right.

The Call of Bellua ✦

At home Hattie headed to the kitchen for an after-school snack. A note on the table explained that Mum had unexpectedly had to go and help Dad at their vet's practice in town.

I'll be back in time for tea, so don't eat all the biscuits!

Mum's message, in her loopy handwriting, made Hattie smile properly for the first time that day as she took a bite from the chocolate biscuit already in her hand.

At least I can put off telling her about the pot for a bit, Hattie thought as she grabbed another biscuit anyway and headed upstairs to her room, the box tucked safely under her arm.

Sitting on her bed, Hattie placed it in front of her on the duvet. She lifted out the broken pot and handle and carefully unwrapped them, trying not to damage the pieces any more than she had already. When she held the handle against the pot, it looked almost perfect again.

Remembering Chloe's advice, she thought, *Could a dab of glue be the answer?* Hattie felt a little hope return, but then she realized she had no idea what kind of glue to use.

As Hattie felt her confidence start to drain away, she heard the front door slam and the familiar heavy tread of her older brother on the stairs.

Of course, she thought. *Peter! He used to make model aeroplanes and stuff so he must know how to fix it.* Maybe Uncle B was right and she *would* find help in an unexpected place!

Hattie called out her brother's name, but she wasn't surprised when he didn't answer. She was about to call him again when a thought hit her: what if Peter not only refused to help her fix the pot but told Mum himself? Or, worse still, used Hattie's secret against her? He could probably make her do his share of the chores for weeks! But another glance at the broken pot told Hattie that she didn't really have a choice.

She called again for Peter and he finally poked his head round her bedroom door. Then it took the offer of a chocolate biscuit for Hattie to entice him to actually enter her room and look at the pot.

Hattie's stomach dropped when he picked up the two parts and shook his head gravely.

'Ooh, that's pretty bad,' he said, tutting loudly. 'Precious china like that needs careful handling, you know.'

'I know that now,' said Hattie impatiently. 'Can you fix it?'

Peter breathed in deeply. 'Hmmm, I might be able to . . . but it'll cost you.'

Knowing she had spent almost everything

in her moneybox on a recent trip to an art shop, Hattie thought fast.

'I'll tidy your room for a week,' she offered hopefully. Without waiting for Peter to answer, and anxious for his help, she added, 'Two weeks, if you do it before Mum gets back – and you promise not to tell her!'

'Deal!' said Peter.

With a cry of gratitude, Hattie hugged her brother – careful not to knock the pot, of course – before he went back to his room.

Hattie lay back on her bed, a wave of relief running through her. As she stretched her arms out above her, the charm bracelet she always wore caught her eye. Hattie sat up quickly and brought it closer, making sure that she was seeing right. The charms were beginning to glow. That could mean only one thing – a creature in the magical Kingdom of Bellua needed her help!

She scrambled off her bed so quickly that she felt a bit dizzy and had to take a deep breath to regain her balance. With no time to lose, she pulled the old vet's bag from under her bed – it was the gateway to the most incredible place she'd ever been.

Which creatures will I meet this time? she

wondered. Sprites, nymphs or maybe more unicorns? The possibilities were endless.

However, as she placed her glowing charm against the lock on the bag, she remembered that returning to the Kingdom of Bellua would mean facing nasty Ivar, King of the Imps, who really didn't like her. She was the one person who could stop his evil plan to take over Bellua, while she protected the creatures he hurt. But a creature needed her now.

She tiptoed to her door and peered out to check the coast was clear. Summoning all her courage, she opened the bag without hesitation.

'I'm coming, Bellua!' she whispered as she looked inside, and immediately found herself tumbling down, down and down . . .

Absent Friends

Hattie grabbed the stone table in the middle of the crystal cave to steady herself as she landed. After her two previous bumpy landings, she was glad that it had been the soles of her trainers rather than her bottom that had broken her fall this time!

Hattie was also pleased that the cave looked exactly the same as before. The walls still glinted with thousands of crystals and the rocky shelves were cluttered with tiny glass potion bottles. The only thing missing was Mith Ickle, the little pink dragon who had greeted her before.

Hattie didn't have time to worry about this. She moved towards an open window at the back of the cave and was dismayed to find hailstones the size of peas showering in. There was a fierce storm outside. The sky was dark with thick clouds and the cave echoed with the sound of the howling wind. Hattie couldn't remember whether she'd forgotten to close the window on her last visit, but part of her wondered if this was King Ivar's doing.

She quickly closed the window and started

to sweep up the hailstones. It wasn't long before she heard a scraping noise at the cave door. Hattie's heart skipped a beat. Surely King Ivar and Immie hadn't come to trouble her already? With caution, Hattie tiptoed to the door and pressed her ear against it.

'Hello?' Hattie said in a smaller voice than she'd intended. 'Who is it?'

She was relieved when the reply came in Mith Ickle's unmistakable sing-song voice. 'It's me: Mith. Can you let me in?'

Remembering how much dragons hate getting wet, Hattie threw open the door and found Mith Ickle panting under the weight of a large leaf that she was holding for shelter.

'I'm so pleased to see you, Mith,' said Hattie with a smile. 'Come in!'

Mith Ickle didn't need any encouragement. However, as she rushed in, the two friends were amazed that the storm stopped the moment Hattie slammed the door shut.

'Typical!' snorted Mith Ickle. 'I'd have been here to greet you if it hadn't been for that storm. I've got bad news from the Fairy Forest. A fairy was trapped by a flower bud and, because she was unable to fly away from the storm, a hailstone hit her delicate wing and tore it. The fairies are sure it's the work of King Ivar and have asked if you might be able to help her as soon as you can.'

'That poor fairy! Let's find out what the cure is and head to the Fairy Forest straight away,' said Hattie.

She moved towards a big red book that was lying on the stone table. Hattie hoped it would lead her to a magical remedy as it had before. Remembering how heavy it was, she was glad she hadn't put it away after helping Lunar the unicorn on her last visit. It usually sat on one of the shelves laden with potion bottles and Hattie had been terrified of knocking them over. After her clumsiness with Mum's china pot at school, she was glad not to face that risk today!

Hattie started to flick through the familiar thick pages of *Healing Magickal Beastes &*

Creatures, looking for a section on fairy ailments. She didn't even blink when the map of Bellua flew out from between the section on water sprites and mermaids, landing light as a feather on the table.

At last Hattie reached a page entitled 'Fairies and their most Common Complaintes'. There were several pictures of fairies with lost wands, with thorns caught in their long hair and even with their wings mysteriously stuck together. It took Hattie a moment to find one that showed a torn wing, but as soon as she did words magically appeared on the page, just as they had before.

Excited to learn what her new adventure might involve, Hattie squinted at the tiny text and began to read aloud:

To avoid risk of harme, the torne wing of a fairy must be sewne with the finest magickal threade, found in a curtained lair that can be discovered only by the keenest of eyes. Know too that this delicate taske requires steady hands.

Hattie could almost hear the voice of the book scolding her as if it knew she was clumsy. *Could it possibly know about the pot?* she wondered.

'Oh dear, this isn't a good start!' she said out loud, but right now she had to concentrate on the injured fairy. She glanced at the map of Bellua beside her and wondered where this magical thread might be hidden. Suddenly Mith Ickle brought Hattie's attention back to the book, tapping with a sharp claw to indicate the verse that was appearing on the page:

The threade to make this fine repair,

Lies in the shimmer spiders' care.

Under a bridge, hidden from view,

'Tis only given to a chosen few.

'Spiders!' Hattie exclaimed with a shudder. 'I always find them a bit creepy, Mith.'

However, this was no time to worry about her own fears. Determined to solve the riddle, Hattie turned to the map of Bellua again and traced a path from the cave until her finger reached a place she remembered from her first adventure: TROLL BRIDGE.

'That must be where the shimmer spiders are – it's the only bridge on the map,' she said.

Her stomach dropped. Getting past the trolls and their riddle had been a challenge last time – and the look on Mith Ickle's face told Hattie that the dragon remembered how they hadn't exactly warmly welcomed *her* either!

Hattie wondered whether they would have to face the trolls if the spiders lived *below* the bridge – but then her whole body shivered at the thought of meeting spiders!

Deciding it was up to her to show Mith Ickle some cheerful confidence, Hattie grabbed the map and turned to the door of the cave.

'Right,' she said purposefully, 'let's go and cure a fairy – trolls or no trolls!'

A Fairy Trap

Hattie and Mith Ickle quickly passed through the Valley of the Guardians and beneath the silver arch that led to Unicorn Meadows. Hattie was delighted to see Lunar, her last patient, galloping through the long grass, his purple and silver coat now glowing richly and his silky tail held high. Close behind him was Themis, the leader of the unicorns.

Hattie couldn't help blushing when the unicorns stopped and bowed their heads towards her in respect. She knew that she would always have the unicorns' support.

Hattie waved to the majestic creatures, then quickly led Mith Ickle out of the meadows and on to the path by the Silvery Stream that would take them to the Fairy Forest.

As soon as they entered the forest, a group of mischievous fairies gathered to play with Mith Ickle and Hattie. Even though they were good-hearted, the fairies had the reputation of being the naughtiest creatures in Bellua. Before Hattie had even had a chance to look for her next patient, she had to deal with two young ones

who were taking it in turns to tug the white
streak that ran through her long dark hair.

'Hey!' cried Hattie, batting them away. The
light streak in her hair, along with the star-
shaped birthmark on her right cheek, marked

Hattie out as a Guardian – and she didn't like anyone teasing them.

The arrival of an older fairy brought their game to a halt. 'Hattie's here to help Titch,' she said, shooing the fairies away. 'We don't want to delay her with your silly games, do we?'

With eyes lowered, the naughty fairies fluttered away, leaving the older fairy to address Hattie.

'Hello, I'm Fizz, and you must be Hattie,' she said, glancing at her hair and cheek. 'Let me take you to meet your patient. Poor Titch is in a very sticky situation!'

Straight away Hattie saw that Fizz was right. Poking out of a tightly closed flower bud, Hattie could see Titch's wings and legs flapping desperately, but her head could not be seen. A group of fairies were hovering nearby, tiny voices urging the bud to release their friend.

'Open up!' they cried. 'Let her go!'

But the bud stayed clamped shut and shook as the fairies tried to help Titch wriggle free.

'How did it happ–' Hattie started to say. Before she could even finish her question, beautiful music filled her ears. It was Mith Ickle!

Hattie knew instantly that her dragon friend

was soothing the flower bud with her song. The watching fairies let out gentle *ooh*s and *aah*s as the bud slowly began to unfurl, spreading its petals and rising on its stalk – releasing a very grateful Titch! The tiny fairy gently fluttered her droopy wings and tried to smooth her messy hair.

'Well done, Mith!' exclaimed Hattie with pride. She walked over to the shivering little fairy and knelt down beside her. 'Titch, could you tell me what happened?' she asked gently.

Weakened by her struggling, Titch's fairy voice was barely more than a whisper and Hattie had to listen carefully.

'I'd just poked my head into the bud to

collect some pollen for a snack when I heard a loud "boo!"' Titch began. 'Then King Ivar appeared right next to me before the flower snapped shut with my head inside!'

Titch paused to wipe a tiny tear before continuing. 'I couldn't see anything, but I could hear his cackling laugh. He said nothing would stop him ruling Bellua now, and within seconds a storm was brewing. Heavy hailstones began to fall all around me. One of them must have ripped my wing here,' she said, sticking a small finger through a hole. 'Fairy magic comes from our wings and I'm sure that King Ivar stole my magic as soon as my wing was torn.' Her voice faltered as she tried to hold in her tears.

Fizz comforted the distressed fairy, whose large, round eyes were still wide with shock. Meanwhile, Hattie leaned forward to inspect Titch's damaged wing more closely. It looked

like it was made from the most delicate lace and was so fine it was almost transparent. Its prettiness was only spoiled by the large hole that the hailstone had made halfway up. Hattie shook her head as she peered through it.

Hovering above Hattie's shoulder, Mith Ickle said, 'Imps can sometimes control the weather. Ivar gained magic when he broke Lunar's horn and I think that gave him the power to create such a great storm.'

Mith Ickle's reasoning made sense to Hattie – and Titch nodded too.

'He did seem pretty pleased with himself. I could hear him laughing the moment the hailstone hit my wing,' said the fairy miserably.

'Don't worry, Titch,' said Hattie. 'Now have a little rest and we'll be back soon to repair that tear. I'll have you flying again in no time! We know exactly what we need – some thread from the shimmer spiders.'

'The shimmer spiders?' asked Fizz with a worried look on her face. She ran a tiny hand nervously through her blonde hair. 'Be careful, Hattie. They can be really grumpy and they creep around sneakily.'

Titch shivered, and Hattie knew it wasn't just because she was cold this time.

Silly Riddles

Hattie and Mith Ickle walked by the Silvery Stream, soon leaving the Fairy Forest behind them and heading for Troll Bridge. Suddenly Hattie thought she could hear a strange splashing sound.

'Can you hear that?' Hattie asked Mith Ickle. 'I think there's something in the water.'

She glanced in the direction of the Silvery Stream, with the Enchanted Orchard on the other side in the distance, and wondered whether they should investigate.

'It's probably just water sprites playing by the dam,' said Mith Ickle. Then she added more loudly, 'Don't get too close, Hattie. The dam is quite unsteady!'

Hattie smiled at her friend's concern. She looked at the stream, but, seeing nothing unusual, she headed back to Mith Ickle.

'Perhaps it *was* water sprites,' she said. 'Come on, Mith – let's hurry to the bridge.'

Mith Ickle reluctantly sped up and Hattie

knew that she wasn't the only one who was dreading seeing the trolls again.

As they approached Troll Bridge, Hattie was relieved to see that there were only a couple of trolls patrolling the top, apparently not interested in their arrival. As she got closer, though, she could see that they were much larger than the ones she'd first met. The trolls turned to watch her and bristled with self-importance.

'It's lucky that we don't need to cross the bridge,' Hattie whispered to Mith.

She was glad that the shimmer spiders' lair was *under* Troll Bridge, rather than on the other side of it. They left the path and headed towards the bank by the bridge, but then Hattie heard the trolls begin to huff and puff to each other.

Not wanting to miss the opportunity of challenging someone, one of them bumbled over to confront her. His chunky build and horns were imposing as he beckoned Hattie towards him with a long, gnarled fingernail. Although Hattie was a little scared by his size, she couldn't help but marvel at his strange leafy headdress.

The second troll then stomped along to join

him. He was a giant troll, like his companion, and his fiery-red hair was fashioned into a point on top of his head.

Neither of them looked very friendly.

Hattie felt Mith Ickle's trembling body curl round her shoulders as the dragon nervously puffed small clouds of smoke about her ears.

'I'm Hattie, Guardian of the creatures of the magical Kingdom of Bellua,' she said as the trolls stopped less than a metre from her. 'We met before. Do you remember?'

Neither troll answered. Instead they began talking to each other as if she wasn't there.

'I'm going to tell her,' said the leafy troll.

'Are you sure?' said his red-haired friend, an uncertain look crossing his heavy brow.

'I think we should.'

'But can we trust her?'

Hattie coughed loudly to remind them she was still there, but it made no difference.

'Can we be sure she really is the Guardian?' the red-haired troll said to his friend.

'I am. I promise I am!' called Hattie. 'Ask me anything: I'll prove it to you!'

Both trolls looked at Hattie, then at each other.

'Read the riddle,' said the leafy troll.

'What riddle?' replied the other.

'The one we use to find out if a Guardian is real or not.' The leafy troll was starting to sound a little impatient.

'But I didn't bring any riddle,' said the red-haired troll, patting himself all over to prove the point.

His friend looked thoughtful for a moment, then clapped his knobbly hands together.

'I know,' he said, 'we'll make one up!'

The other troll looked doubtful, but his friend was on a roll.

Hattie tried not to laugh as each troll took a turn at composing a line of the riddle:

'*We know when a Guardian's true,*' began the leafy troll.

'*They show a mark – or is it two?*' added the red-haired one.

'*Or it might be three or even four.*'

'*So tell us, Guardian, what's your score?*' ended the red-haired troll, a look of triumph in his bulbous eyes.

'Two,' answered Hattie confidently, pointing first to the white streak in her hair and then to the star-shaped birthmark on her cheek.

The two trolls looked at each other, then the red-haired one nodded a little uncertainly before the leafy one spoke again.

'Yes, two marks of the Guardian – that must be right,' he said, before moving a step closer.

Hattie felt Mith Ickle's breathing quicken.

'Beware,' he whispered, sending a waft of foul-smelling breath in her direction. 'We've seen the evil King Ivar around here, loitering near our bridge with that blue-haired imp. We couldn't hear what was said, Guardian, but he was telling her something, pointing out this and that and whispering in her horrible impy ear. Whatever she said back made Ivar clap his nasty hands with glee. The two of them looked really happy when they ran off together, cackling and squealing. So you watch out!'

'I wonder if that splashing sound we heard earlier was something to do with Ivar and Immie,' Hattie said worriedly.

The trolls turned on their horny heels and headed back to their sentry positions on the bridge.

'My last line was definitely the best!' she heard the red-haired troll say.

'But I put in all the numbers to confuse her!' argued the other.

'It's lucky troll riddles are pretty easy to solve,' Hattie laughed as Mith Ickle uncurled herself from her shoulders, and they both watched the still-bickering trolls clumsily clamber back on to the bridge. 'We don't have time to worry about what King Ivar and Immie said. We'll just have to be even more cautious than usual. Right now, we have some very important thread to find!'

Slippery Stones

Glad that the trolls were no longer bothering them, Hattie and Mith walked towards the bank of the stream. For the first time, Hattie had a proper look at the trolls' stone bridge. She gazed in wonder at the intricate patterns that had been sculpted into its large arch. However, Hattie knew that she had no time to marvel at the beauty of Bellua.

The bank on which they stood was very steep. Rough, mossy stones led down to the stream and Hattie could make out a fine curtain stretching down from the lower edge of the bridge's arch, just skimming the sparkling water that flowed beneath it.

'That must be the shimmer spiders' lair!' exclaimed Hattie. 'But how do we get to it?'

The only way to reach it was to climb down to the rocks by the water's edge. But, remembering how careless she'd been with her mum's china pot, Hattie was worried that she might be as clumsy now. The path looked rather slippery!

Taking a deep breath, Hattie started to clamber down the rocky bank.

'Be careful, Hattie!' called Mith.

'I'm fine,' Hattie called back. 'You stay there, Mith. I know you don't like getting wet!'

However, as she made a leap from one moss-covered stone to another, disaster struck! Her trainer slid on the moss as soon as she landed and her body arched backwards, her second foot uselessly pedalling through the air. Hattie knew she was about to tumble into the stream!

Just in time, Hattie saw a streak of familiar pink. Mith Ickle had rushed up and nudged her from behind, shooting a burst of fire below her feet.

'It's safe here, Hattie,' called Mith Ickle, using her snout to point Hattie's trainer towards a flat brownish stone.

When she stepped on to it, Hattie found that it was perfectly dry and not at all slippery.

'Thank you so much, Mith,' said Hattie. 'You're so clever to use your fire to dry out the moss!'

Before the dragon could answer, Hattie let out another cry: 'Oh, we're here! The spiders' lair!'

With Mith Ickle beaming beside her, Hattie looked in awe at the beautiful shimmering curtain. It seemed to be woven from spider thread – and it was the most intricate, glistening cobweb she'd ever seen!

Hattie cautiously reached towards the curtain, but as she touched it the thread immediately stuck to her finger and was almost impossible to rub off. She cried out and Mith Ickle tried to help her pull loose from the web. They called out for help, hoping the giant trolls might hear them, but no one came.

All of a sudden, a thin black leg pushed through the shimmering curtain, then another, followed by two more. Each leg ended in a sharp claw, and Hattie flinched as they revealed themselves to be attached to a round, shiny

black body, topped with a head bearing five swivelling eyes – three small ones above two large – that peered through the curtain at them.

Hattie looked at the spider curiously as he emerged. She couldn't believe she was meeting a spider her own size! Remembering how she always jumped when spiders darted unexpectedly across the floor at home, Hattie convinced herself that she was more surprised by the spider's sudden appearance than terrified by his size. It helped that he was wearing a pair of round metal-rimmed glasses that reminded her of her old maths teacher – they made the spider look intelligent rather than scary.

The spider brought his four front legs together, a gesture that Hattie thought must be a greeting.

Hattie put her own hands together too. 'Hello, I'm Hattie, Guardian of the creatures of the magical Kingdom of Bellua,' she said, her voice quivering slightly.

'I know,' replied the spider in a gruff voice. 'You'd better come inside,' he said, sweeping the curtain aside. Hattie noticed that the thread didn't stick to him. 'Enter quickly, so we can safely seal our lair again,' said the spider as Hattie darted through the gap, Mith Ickle close behind.

The spiders' lair was less gloomy than Hattie

had expected. Light bounced off the spindles of shimmering spider thread that were lined up along its walls.

'I'm Onyx,' said the spider who had let her in, 'the chief of the shimmer spiders.' Then his eyes swivelled menacingly towards Mith Ickle, who had curled herself round Hattie's shoulders again, so that Hattie could feel her warm body shaking with fear. 'Who let that dragon in?' he growled.

'She's with me,' said Hattie. 'She won't cause you any trouble, I promise.'

'So *you* say,' replied Onyx, though Hattie didn't think he sounded convinced. 'Well, it would be difficult to leave now,' he continued, waving a long clawed leg towards the lair's entrance. 'Your friend may stay.'

Hattie turned back and saw that a whole army of spiders was already busy restoring the

curtain that blocked off the outside world. The sight of so many spiders scrambling around made Hattie feel a little shaky again, but she concentrated on her relief that Onyx was going to let Mith Ickle stay.

'Explain the purpose of your visit, Guardian,' said Onyx sternly.

So, with Onyx's large dark eyes never leaving her face, Hattie explained about Titch's torn wing and how she needed to find the finest magical thread to repair it.

Onyx nodded his head slowly and Hattie hoped he might just hand her the thread she needed. But then the spider spoke again. 'Our thread is rare and precious,' he said, using a leg to push his glasses a little higher up his face. 'We don't give it to anyone, not even the Guardian of Bellua. You must show you deserve even the smallest length of it. Come this way and I will set you a task to prove your worth.'

Hattie had no choice but to follow the scuttling spider deeper into the lair.

In the Lair

Before Onyx revealed Hattie's challenge, he explained how shimmer spiders produced their magical thread.

'Our thread is fragile because we spin it so finely,' he said. 'It is for this reason that the spiders work in pairs. While one spins the thread, another winds it carefully on to a wooden spindle, which can be stored for future use.'

Glancing around the lair, Hattie spotted several pairs of spiders doing exactly this.

Staring Hattie unblinkingly in the eyes, Onyx continued. 'For your task you must wind two perfect spindles of thread. If you succeed, the second of these will be yours to take away. The thread you handle will not be sticky; we only add the sticky coating to the curtain as extra protection. Be warned, however: the thread is most delicate, and the slightest pull will cause it to snap. I will allow just one mistake. If your thread breaks or tangles more than once, you will leave empty-handed.'

Hattie looked again at the spiders around her, who were busy spinning thread with their thin, clawed legs. She peered down at her fingers. Could she keep them steady enough to handle the fragile thread? An image of Mum's broken pot flashed before her and Hattie blinked hard to put the earlier mishap out of her mind.

Hattie nodded to show Onyx that she accepted the challenge. Taking a deep breath, she followed him to a far corner of the lair.

'This is Jet,' said Onyx, introducing Hattie to a spider. 'Jet is one of our younger spiders and so has the energy to produce thread more easily than some. He will suffer less if any of his thread is wasted.'

'But I won't –' Hattie began.

Onyx dismissed her with a wave of one of his spindly legs and a loud snort. 'Many have failed this task. And humans –' he looked Hattie up and down, sneering – 'are hardly equipped for this work.'

Taking the spindle from Onyx was the first challenge. It was so fine Hattie needed a firm grip to stop it from slipping out of her fingers before she had even begun. Finally, with Jet positioned in front of her, she took hold of the end of thread he produced and began to wind.

With Mith Ickle singing words of encouragement, Hattie was surprised and delighted to see the thread quickly build up on

the spindle. She couldn't help thinking that Mith Ickle's delicate claws would have done the job more easily, but she was pleased that her fingers seemed to be picking up a rhythm. Even Onyx's harsh stare began to relax slightly after a while. But then things took a turn for the worse . . .

Just as Hattie was beginning to feel confident, the shimmering thread caught the light that filtered in through the curtain at the lair's entrance. It glinted so brightly that Hattie's eyes watered and without thinking she raised a hand to wipe away the unwelcome tears – jerking the precious thread!

A gasp from Mith Ickle immediately told

Hattie what she had done. One glance at the snapped thread made her stomach lurch just as it had when she had broken Mum's china pot that morning! Her heart thumping, she turned to Onyx to see what he would say.

'You have one more chance to prove yourself, Guardian,' said the chief spider gruffly. 'But only one.'

Hattie knew the pressure was really on now. Concentrating, she steadied her hands and began to wind again, round and round and round, until the spindle was full.

Onyx scuttled forward to judge her work. 'Let's see,' he said, taking the spindle and holding it right up to his glasses. Hattie waited nervously for his verdict. 'Yes, a good enough job, I suppose,' he continued. 'You have passed this first test.'

Any relief Hattie felt was short-lived. As Jet handed the full spindle to another spider for safekeeping, Onyx produced another empty one and passed it to Hattie. 'Fill this with care and it will be yours,' he said, before settling back to watch her try.

The second spindle seemed to fill up more quickly than the first, Hattie thought as she wound the bright thread, taking care to avoid lowering or raising her hands too far this time. Eventually Onyx stepped back and took the spindle for inspection. Hattie watched him with bated breath.

At last, having turned the spindle every which way, Onyx cleared his throat.

'A full spindle,' he declared. Hattie allowed the trace of a smile to cross her lips before he continued in a noticeably softer voice, 'And not only full but perfectly wound. There are spiders here who fail to wind our thread as neatly as this, Hattie. Should you ever stop being the Guardian, I would employ you here.'

Mith Ickle gave a little whoop of joy, congratulating Hattie excitedly. Hattie couldn't help beaming as she thanked Onyx and attempted a small bow of respect.

Although Hattie felt relieved that her time in the claustrophobic lair was almost over, she put aside the impulse to leave as quickly as she could. When Onyx handed her the precious spindle of thread she thanked him profusely, before saying her goodbyes to Jet and all the other spiders.

Mith Ickle was leading the way to the entrance when Hattie heard a loud gushing sound echo around the dark chamber. One glance back told Hattie it was serious. Every spider's eyes were wide open and fixed in terror.

Flash Flood!

'The dam must have burst!' shouted Onyx, his calm voice replaced by one of urgency and panic. 'To work, spiders, to work!'

At their chief's command all the spiders scuttled hurriedly around the lair, moving spindles of thread to safety, before disappearing into nooks and crannies in the walls. Soon, with the gushing noise growing louder around them, only Hattie and Mith Ickle were left.

Water had swept away the curtain at the entrance and was rushing into the lair. The little dragon flapped her wings frantically, desperately trying to keep herself dry. Hattie, ankle deep in water, looked around for an escape route. She would never be able to reach the crevices that the spiders had scattered to!

'You go, Mith!' Hattie called. 'Fly out while you can. Don't worry about me.'

She saw a look of uncertainty cross her little friend's face.

'I'll be OK,' Hattie said to reassure her. 'Only my trainers are wet so far – and I'm a pretty good swimmer. Take this and get yourself out of here.'

She held out the precious spindle of spider thread and Mith Ickle didn't need any further encouragement.

'I'll go and get help!' the dragon called as she disappeared through the lair's opening, the spindle gripped tightly in her claws.

Hattie had to put her fear aside and find a way out of the lair before it flooded completely.

With cold water now at her knees, she waded towards the way out. The water was gushing in and the climb up the rocky bank seemed impossible. With unsteady footing, she reached the flat stone by the entrance to the lair and clung tightly to the side of the bridge's arch. Slowly losing her grip, Hattie looked around frantically. If she was careful, she could get to a higher stone and then climb on to the arch's small ledge.

Concentrating hard, Hattie was able to heave herself on to it. Although she was relieved to be out of the water, Hattie could see that the stream beneath her was rising quickly. She wasn't out of danger yet!

Hattie held on and weighed up her options.

I could try to reach the edge of the bridge and swing myself up, she thought.

But when she judged the distance she realized it was too far away.

Oh dear, what am I going to do now? she wondered.

A voice from above startled her. 'Na, na,

ne na, na! You'll never get out of there, Hattie B!'

Hattie looked up to see Immie's head hanging over the bridge, her blue hair dangling down.

'I broke the dam and the water won't stop rising for a *loooooong* time. You're going to be stuck on that ledge FOREVER. Hope you like getting wet!'

Before Hattie could say anything back, the imp's head disappeared and her teasing voice was replaced by another loud gush of water.

Sensing that the water level was about to rise again dramatically, Hattie knew she didn't

have any more time to plan her escape. She would have to jump.

She was about to make the dangerous leap when something caught her eye in the water below: a large log. It looked as if it was being swept straight towards her.

As the log got closer, Hattie realized it wasn't so much drifting in her direction as being guided. Inching as close to the edge of the ledge as she dared, she peered down and was amazed to see a group of water sprites arranged in a neat V formation behind the log as they propelled it through the water. Hattie could see their little legs kicking with determination, their iridescent hair flowing behind them in the fast-moving water.

The sprites beckoned Hattie to jump, but the gap was too big. Hattie knew she wouldn't make it.

'Can you get any closer?' she called desperately, hoping they could hear her.

To Hattie's relief, they kicked hard again and managed to steer the log close enough for Hattie to risk a jump.

'Coming in one – two – three!' shouted Hattie, before her soggy trainers landed on the wood with a damp thud.

'Thank you so, so much for rescuing me,'

she said to the flotilla of water sprites, who
were now guiding the log to the bank. 'Seems
Immie got it wrong again!'

She was soon close enough to the bank to

step on to dry land again, where an excited Mith Ickle was waiting for her.

'Oh, Hattie, thank goodness you're safe,' said the little dragon, swooping down to blow warm air on to Hattie's sodden clothes.

'All thanks to the water sprites,' replied Hattie, turning back to her helpers, whose tiny arms were raised out of the water in farewell waves.

'Goodbye! And thanks again!' Hattie called as she watched the creatures speed away through the water.

'Did you see Immie, Mith? It was Ivar and Immie who broke the dam! But it looks

like their plan to stop me has failed again.'
A rush of confidence surged through Hattie.
'We need to hurry back to the Fairy Forest
and sort out poor Titch's torn wing. You have
got the –'

'Thread?' finished Mith Ickle, holding up
the spindle for Hattie to see. 'Safe, sound and
perfectly dry!'

'Let's go!' said Hattie with a smile.

However, as they headed to the path,
something caught her eye. Floating above
them in Bellua's magical sky was a strange dark
spot. It was too high up for her to distinguish
any details but unusual enough to make her

take note. Hattie frowned, but decided there wasn't time to worry about it.

As she hurried with Mith Ickle towards the Fairy Forest, Hattie felt her heart thumping in her chest. Would they get to Titch without any meddling this time, or would her bravery be put to the test yet again?

Face to Face

Back in the Fairy Forest, Hattie found Titch curled up on a bed of soft leaves. Two young fairies were fanning her with petals, while Fizz was perched on the edge of Titch's bed, gently stroking her forehead.

'We've tried to give her some nectar, but she's too frail to drink it,' explained Fizz.

Hattie held up the spindle of magical thread

proudly. 'It's OK, Titch,' she said. 'I'll be able to fix your torn wing as soon as we get back to the cave. Are you ready to go?'

However, one look at Titch's tired eyes and tiny legs told Hattie that the poor fairy wasn't strong enough to walk anywhere.

'You could hitch a ride on Mith,' Hattie said. But Titch twisted her face and she could see that the injured fairy wasn't keen.

'She's very friendly, I promise,' said Hattie. Titch still didn't look convinced, though. 'OK, how about you sit on my shoulder?' she suggested instead. 'You can hold on to my hair.'

With Titch carefully placed on her right
shoulder, Hattie set off for the cave, soon
leaving the Fairy Forest behind to rejoin the

path by the Silvery Stream. Flapping alongside her, Mith Ickle tried to cheer Titch up by chattering away.

As they walked, Hattie couldn't help but think about her lucky escape from the flood.

'What do you think Ivar will do now Immie's failed to stop me again, Mith?' Hattie asked, a slight wobble in her voice. 'I'm worried he'll have something even worse than a flash flood up his sleeve now.'

At that moment there was a loud spatter on the ground in front of them. They all glanced around to see where it had come from.

'Uh-oh,' said Mith Ickle. 'It looks like it won't be too long before you find out!'

Hattie followed Mith Ickle's gaze and saw that the dark spot she had seen in the sky earlier had moved closer – close enough to see exactly what it was. There was no mistaking the old impish face, which was twisted into a menacing scowl. King Ivar!

Hattie felt her mouth fall open in silent surprise. She took in the Imp King's small squinty eyes, large pointy ears and crooked teeth. Wrapped round him was a long greenish-brown cloak, its collar turned up and the hem trailing into the sky behind him as he hovered, his small bony wings flapping hard.

'Looks like he's already learned to fly then,' said Mith Ickle, breaking the silence.

'Yes,' agreed Hattie quietly. 'He must have stolen some of your magical power, Titch, just as you suspected.'

Titch nodded her head weakly as they watched the flying Imp King reach inside his cloak. He pulled out a small sack and swooped towards them, his evil cackle filling the air. Ivar plunged a hand into the sack and released a handful of hard purple berries, which rained down on the path in front of them.

'Bruiseberries!' shouted Mith Ickle. 'Avoid them if you can, Hattie. They'll cause painful bruises if they hit you.'

Hattie jumped clear of the next handful,

only to find that every berry landed with a splash in the Silvery Stream.

'He needs to sort out his aim!' laughed Hattie when his next handful also missed them and landed among a pile of rocks beside the stream. 'Or maybe he needs more flying practice,' she added, looking up to see him desperately flapping his tiny imp wings as he tried to follow their progress along the path.

To her horror, though, King Ivar seemed to quickly work out how to point himself towards the small group, and the bruiseberries started landing closer and closer. Hattie knew she had to protect Mith Ickle and Titch.

Suddenly she had a flash of inspiration. Giving Titch little choice in the matter, she handed her to Mith Ickle with a brief apology and began scrabbling around on the ground until she found a twig that was long and bendy enough to satisfy her.

'What are you doing, Hattie?' asked Mith Ickle, looking confused.

'Showing that nasty Ivar that he won't stop us getting to the cave this time,' replied Hattie confidently.

'With a twig?' Mith Ickle looked positively mystified now.

'Think of it as a berry catapult!' said Hattie. She had remembered how Peter had once spent a whole afternoon picking cherries off the tree in the garden and showing her how to fire them across the lawn.

Picking a bruiseberry off the ground, Hattie put it firmly in the centre of the twig, pulled the wood back and whispered to herself, 'Keep your eye on your target and FIRE!'

She fixed her glare on King Ivar and released the berry, sending it soaring into the sky.

'Wow!' exclaimed Mith Ickle and Titch in unison as the fruit flew through the air in a perfect arc, reaching its target effortlessly.

Howls and yowls of pain echoed around them as the bruiseberry hit King Ivar square in the chest and sent him whirling through the

sky, looping the loop in the opposite direction
to Hattie's route to the cave.

'Quick, let's get away from here!' called Hattie.
'If we hurry, we should get to safety in Dragon's
Valley before he recovers enough to chase us.'

The dragon and fairy didn't need any encouragement. Within seconds they were following her.

King Ivar's furious voice boomed around them. 'YOU'LL PAY FOR THIS, HATTIE B! THIS ISN'T THE LAST YOU'LL SEE OF ME! I'LL GET YOU NEXT TIME!'

Mith Ickle was shaken – and there was a wobble in her voice as she sang the special song that opened the entrance to Dragon's Valley. The dragons they saw inside greeted Mith Ickle and Hattie warmly, as the two friends quickly made their way to the other side of the valley.

'Right, Titch, let's see if I can bring back your fairy flight,' said Hattie as they finally entered the Guardian's cave.

She tried to ignore her nerves about the task ahead, but her hands already felt unsteady . . .

A Stitch in Time

Hattie lowered Titch gently on to the vet's table, where the red leather book was still lying open.

The spiders' magickal threade may be sewne only with a needle equally fine, read Hattie. She'd heard of finding a needle in a haystack – but in a magical cave? She didn't know where to start!

After looking in various nooks and crannies, Hattie began to doubt she would ever spot a needle delicate enough to take the magical thread. As she looked sympathetically at Titch leaning wearily against the bowl of instruments on the table, she wondered if she had missed the most obvious place. On her two last adventures Hattie had found a useful dropper, a spoon and even a pen in the glass bowl.

Pulling out an old leather pouch nestled at the bottom, Hattie was delighted to find it contained a bright silver needle. But when she looked at it more closely her joy began to fade. The hole in it was tiny. How would

she ever be able to push the spider thread
through it?

After several failed attempts and more than

one groan of despair, Mith Ickle came to the rescue. She flew over with a long-handled magnifying glass clasped in her claws.

'I found this at the back of the cave,' she said, holding it above the needle so that Hattie could see the hole at several times its size.

It took a couple more attempts before Hattie's hands were steady enough to pass the thread through, but at last she was ready to get to work.

With Mith Ickle holding the magnifying glass over Titch's torn wing, Hattie found it easier to sew up the tear than she had thought. In and out she went with the fine needle, careful not to pull the fragile thread too hard.

With each stitch, the thread glowed with all the colours of the rainbow and Hattie was thrilled it seemed to be working its magic. Her first stitches may not have been completely straight, but once she had done a few she began to relax, settling into a steady rhythm and producing a growing line of neat stitches.

'You sew well, Hattie,' said Mith Ickle, looking on approvingly.

'My grandma taught me,' replied Hattie, remembering the small felt purses that Grandma had helped her and Peter to make one long summer holiday several years ago. Grandma had insisted on careful, even stitches and made them practise until they got it right – although it hadn't stopped all the coins falling out of the gaps in Peter's finished purse. Hattie smiled at the memory. With the tear in Titch's wing almost repaired, Hattie realized that Grandma had passed on a very useful skill.

Finally Hattie declared the wing to be completely fixed. Titch nervously moved it to and fro, testing to see if it was back to full strength. At first nothing much happened, then Hattie noticed the part she had sewn begin to twinkle. She was amazed to see a wash of delicate, glistening colours emerge and spread through the whole wing, until it looked like the finest sliver of mother-of-pearl.

A beaming Titch beat both her wings firmly and lifted herself confidently into the air, a shimmer of light following her.

'That's . . . beautiful!' said Hattie with a sigh.

Hattie returned the needle to its pouch for safekeeping while the delighted fairy flitted around the cave, releasing small puffs of fairy dust with every wingbeat, so that the cave took on an even more magical glow than usual. As Titch approached the door, she released a huge cloud of fairy dust, which floated away to reveal a gleaming fairy charm.

'It's for you!' called Titch. 'Thank you for helping me, Hattie. I'll tell all my friends to never pull your hair again!'

Hattie laughed and walked over to pick up

the pretty charm. 'Goodbye, Titch. Look after those wings!'

'I will,' replied Titch. 'Goodbye, Hattie! Goodbye, Mith!' And with a friendly wave and a farewell puff of fairy dust she flew through the open door and back to Bellua.

All that remained was for Hattie to store the leftover spider thread. She put it in a small jar, labelled it and placed it next to the sunray flowers and crushed moonstone that she had saved from her last two adventures. Hattie found herself counting them proudly: *one, two, three* lots of magical ingredients added to the Guardian's stores. She was really thrilled at her success in this strange land, far away from her family and friends — and just about anything that was familiar!

'Time to go then, Hattie?' asked Mith Ickle sadly.

Hattie nodded. 'But you know I'll be back again,' she said, patting her friend gently on the head. 'I'm already looking forward to our next adventure – even facing King Ivar. Especially if he's still flying all over the place like a bird with a blindfold!'

Mith Ickle and Hattie both giggled as they remembered watching King Ivar as he had tried to control his weak new wings. But Hattie noticed a look of concern cross Mith Ickle's face.

'I'll be your eyes and ears in Bellua,' said the

little dragon, passing her the vet's bag. 'Goodbye, Hattie – until next time.'

'Bye, Mith, take care!' replied Hattie. Then she opened the sparkling bag and peered inside. In a matter of moments she was tumbling back home.

In a Fix

Hattie found herself back on her warm, safe bed, clutching the pretty little fairy charm. She attached it to her bracelet, then pushed the vet's bag, now returned to dull leather, back into its hiding place under her bed. Seeing the fairy charm dangling daintily, she thought of Titch's repaired wing and the row of tiny neat stitches she had managed to sew. If only she had taken as much care handling Mum's china pot!

Hattie was just wondering whether Mum was home yet when her bedroom door creaked open and Peter's smiling face appeared round it. He proudly held up Mum's pot, so that a delighted Hattie could see that it had two handles again.

'Oh thanks, Peter! You might have saved my life!' she said.

Peter shrugged. 'It was dead easy to fix,' he said. 'I did it in no time. I used some old modelling glue I found in my drawer. I bet Mum won't even notice, unless I accidentally mention it, that is . . .'

'You wouldn't!' cried Hattie, before spotting

the smirk on her brother's face. 'I won't tidy your room if you do! In fact, I'll *accidentally* mess it up instead.'

Peter laughed and ruffled Hattie's hair. Then before she could say another word he had bounded out of the room.

Holding the pot tightly, Hattie looked more closely at Peter's repair. Knowing that no time had passed in the real world while she was in Bellua, she guessed that Peter was right: it must have only taken him a few minutes to fix – the time it had taken her to find the vet's bag under her bed and put it back again probably.

It looked like he'd done a good job. Uncle B had been right – she *had* found help where she'd least expected it. Not only had Peter helped her but the sprites in Bellua had saved her from the flood. Hattie wondered whether Uncle B had already known what would happen when she'd bumped into him, before deciding that that couldn't be true. *Could it?*

The join in the pot was hardly visible, although on closer inspection Hattie noticed that a tiny piece of the flower design had chipped off. Remembering her success with Titch's wing, Hattie felt sure this was something she could sort out herself. She sat at her desk, grabbed a blue felt-tip pen and dabbed a little ink on to the pot, delighted to see the chip virtually disappear.

Almost certain that Mum wouldn't even notice the pot had been broken in the first place, Hattie wondered if she could get away with not telling her at all. But wasn't it wrong to say nothing? Maybe now that she'd fixed it she should own up and apologize. The more she thought about it, the more she was sure that was the right thing to do. Hattie was planning how she'd tell Mum when the shrill ring of the phone sailed up the stairs.

Knowing that Mum and Dad were both still at work and that Peter would ignore any phone other than his own mobile, Hattie bounded down with the pot to answer it.

'Do you think you'll still get into trouble with your mum?' Chloe asked, once Hattie had explained with relief that Peter had glued the handle back on.

'It looks pretty good so I hope not,' replied Hattie. 'But I'm not going to bring anything like that into school again. I'm going to do my project on the *skills* that get passed from generation to generation, not the *objects*.'

'Like what?' asked Chloe, not sounding at all convinced.

'Like sewing. My grandma taught me to sew and I'll pass that skill on one day,' explained Hattie.

'But I've never seen you sew *anything*!' Chloe giggled, and Hattie thought she'd better laugh too.

'Well, you might one day, you never know,' she said, thinking of Titch's neatly sewn fairy wing and really wishing she could tell Chloe about it.

The two girls had just started discussing the wedding dress that Victoria Frost had taken into school when Chloe remembered it was time for her piano lesson and the two friends said a quick goodbye.

Hattie put the phone down with a sigh and went back to her room.

She felt sad that she couldn't share her adventures in Bellua with her best friend. She and Chloe normally told each other *everything*, but Hattie knew she couldn't say anything about the amazing magical creatures she'd met. Or describe her victories over King Ivar and Immie. Or share her fears about what the nasty imps might do next time. The only thing that made it bearable was knowing she had a true friend in Mith Ickle, who she hoped would always be there on her adventures.

Holding her bracelet up to the light, Hattie looked at the charms on it: a star, a dragon, a unicorn and now a fairy. What would she add to it next? Hattie couldn't even begin to

imagine, but as she heard Mum's key turn in the lock she hoped she wouldn't have to wait too long to find out.

Read
The Mermaid's Tail
to see what happens next!

Another creature needs Hattie's help in the
Kingdom of Bellua! A mermaid has lost the colour
in her tail, and Hattie knows who has stolen it –
evil King Ivar of the Imps.

Hattie must travel across the desert
to collect the mermaid's medicine.
Will she make it back in time to save her?

Hattie's World

Hattie meets lots of new people on her adventures but who are you most like?

1) What your best friend loves most about you is ...

a) How brave you are when everyone else is feeling scared
b) How you always think of her first
c) How much you make her laugh

2) You're in a race and the girl in front of you stumbles, hurting her ankle. What do you do?

a) Stop and support her under her shoulder so her foot needn't touch the floor. Then keep running until you both manage to cross the line.
b) Sit down next to her and wait together until the race is finished and help comes.
c) Keep running. The faster you get to the end and win the race, the faster you can ask for help.

3) Who would you be most likely to tell a secret ...?

a) No one! You've been trusted to keep a secret and
you're going to do it, no matter what.
b) Your best friend. You know you can trust her.
c) Everybody! Secrets are no fun unless lots of people know them!

4) Your favourite colour is ...

a) Healing green
b) Girly pink
c) Sassy red

5) When you grow up, you want to be ...

a) A vet
b) A writer
c) The boss of your own company

Answers

Mostly As – You're Hattie! Brave and quirky,
you love animals and adventure.

Mostly Bs – You're Chloe! Loyal, kind, thoughtful
and always looking out for your friends.

Mostly Cs – You're Victoria! Sassy, confident and prepared
to do whatever you have to do to get what you want!

Spot the Difference

Can you spot the five differences between these pictures of Hattie B and Chloe?

Bright and shiny and sizzling with fun stuff . . .

puffin.co.uk

WEB FUN

UNIQUE and exclusive digital content!
Podcasts, photos, Q&A, Day in the Life of, interviews
and much more, from Eoin Colfer, Cathy Cassidy,
Allan Ahlberg and Meg Rosoff to Lynley Dodd!

WEB NEWS

The **Puffin Blog** is packed with posts and photos from
Puffin HQ and special guest bloggers. You can also sign up
to our monthly newsletter **Puffin Beak Speak**

WEB CHAT

Discover something new EVERY month –
books, competitions and treats galore

WEBBED FEET

(Puffins have funny little feet and
brightly coloured beaks)

Point your mouse our way today!

It all started with a Scarecrow

Puffin is over seventy years old.
Sounds ancient, doesn't it? But Puffin has never been
so lively. We're always on the lookout for the next big
idea, which is how it began all those years ago.

Penguin Books was a big idea from the mind of
a man called Allen Lane, who in 1935 invented
the quality paperback and changed the world.
**And from great Penguins, great Puffins grew,
changing the face of children's books forever.**

The first four Puffin Picture Books were hatched in 1940 and the
first Puffin story book featured a man with broomstick arms called
Worzel Gummidge. In 1967 Kaye Webb, Puffin Editor, started the
Puffin Club, promising to **'make children into readers'**.
She kept that promise and over 200,000 children became devoted
Puffineers through their quarterly instalments of *Puffin Post*.

Many years from now, we hope you'll look back and
remember Puffin with a smile. **No matter what your age
or what you're into, there's a Puffin for everyone.**
The possibilities are endless, but one thing is for sure:
whether it's a picture book or a paperback, a sticker book
or a hardback, **if it's got that little Puffin
on it – it's bound to be good.**